Dear Parent:
Your child's love of reading starts here!

Every child learns to read in a different way and at his or her own speed. Some go back and forth between reading levels and read favorite books again and again. Others read through each level in order. You can help your young reader improve and become more confident by encouraging his or her own interests and abilities. From books your child reads with you to the first books he or she reads alone, there are I Can Read Books for every stage of reading:

SHARED READING
Basic language, word repetition, and whimsical illustrations, ideal for sharing with your emergent reader

BEGINNING READING
Short sentences, familiar words, and simple concepts for children eager to read on their own

READING WITH HELP
Engaging stories, longer sentences, and language play for developing readers

READING ALONE
Complex plots, challenging vocabulary, and high-interest topics for the independent reader

ADVANCED READING
Short paragraphs, chapters, and exciting themes for the perfect bridge to chapter books

I Can Read Books have introduced children to the joy of reading since 1957. Featuring award-winning authors and illustrators and a fabulous cast of beloved characters, I Can Read Books set the standard for beginning readers.

A lifetime of discovery begins with the magical words **"I Can Read!"**

Visit www.icanread.com for information
on enriching your child's reading experience.

For Poppy, who is an
exceptional reader
—J.O.C.

For my three little sisters,
Erica, Lisa, and Jacquie:
"Stop licking the bowl!"
—R.P.G.

I Can Read Book® is a trademark of HarperCollins Publishers.

Fancy Nancy: JoJo and Daddy Bake a Cake
Text copyright © 2017 by Jane O'Connor
Illustrations copyright © 2017 by Robin Preiss Glasser
All rights reserved. Manufactured in China.
No part of this book may be used or reproduced in any manner whatsoever without written permission except in the case
of brief quotations embodied in critical articles and reviews. For information address HarperCollins Children's Books,
a division of HarperCollins Publishers, 195 Broadway, New York, NY 10007.
www.icanread.com

Library of Congress Control Number: 2016960404
ISBN 978-0-06-237802-6 (trade bdg.) — ISBN 978-0-06-237801-9 (pbk.)

Typography by Jeff Shake
17 18 19 20 21 SCP 10 9 8 7 6 5 4 3 2 1 ❖ First Edition

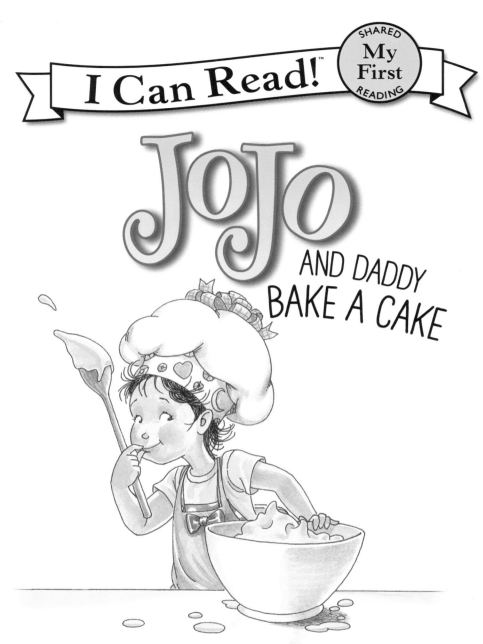

JoJo
AND DADDY
BAKE A CAKE

by Jane O'Connor
cover illustration by Robin Preiss Glasser
interior illustrations by Rick Whipple

HARPER
An Imprint of HarperCollinsPublishers

I am baking a cake.
Daddy is my helper.

"Who is the cake for?"
Daddy asks.

I say, "It's a surprise."
Then I zip my lips.

We mix lots of stuff
into a bowl.

I let Daddy help.

He is a good helper.

Mommy finds the cake pans.
"Who is the cake for?"
Mommy asks.

I say, "It's a surprise."
Then I zip my lips.

I pour the cake mix
into the pans.

I let Daddy help me again.
He is a very good helper.
Daddy puts the pans
into the oven.

Oh look!

It's Freddy.

He wants to play.

I tell him,

"I am busy.

I am baking a cake."

"Who is the cake for?"
Freddy asks.

I say, "It's a surprise."

Then I zip my lips.

Freddy helps Daddy and me
make frosting.
Now I have two helpers.

The frosting is good.
It's very, very good!

Soon the pans come out
of the oven.

Nancy smells the cake.

"Who is it for?"
asks my sister.
I say, "It's a surprise."
Then I zip my lips.

Nancy helps frost the cake.

I have three helpers now.
We make the cake fancy.

Daddy says,

"Now can you tell us

who the cake is for?"

"No. Not yet," I say.
Then I zip my lips.

Daddy has to take Frenchy
for a walk.
Freddy has to go home.

Only Nancy is left.

So I unzip my lips.

I tell Nancy my secret.

She helps with one last thing.

After dinner
I bring out the cake.

Daddy sees it.
He is so surprised!
It is for him!

"Because you are
the best daddy—
and the best helper—
in the world!"